Travel Adventures

The Serengeti

Counting

Dona Herweck Rice

Zero rain falls.

0

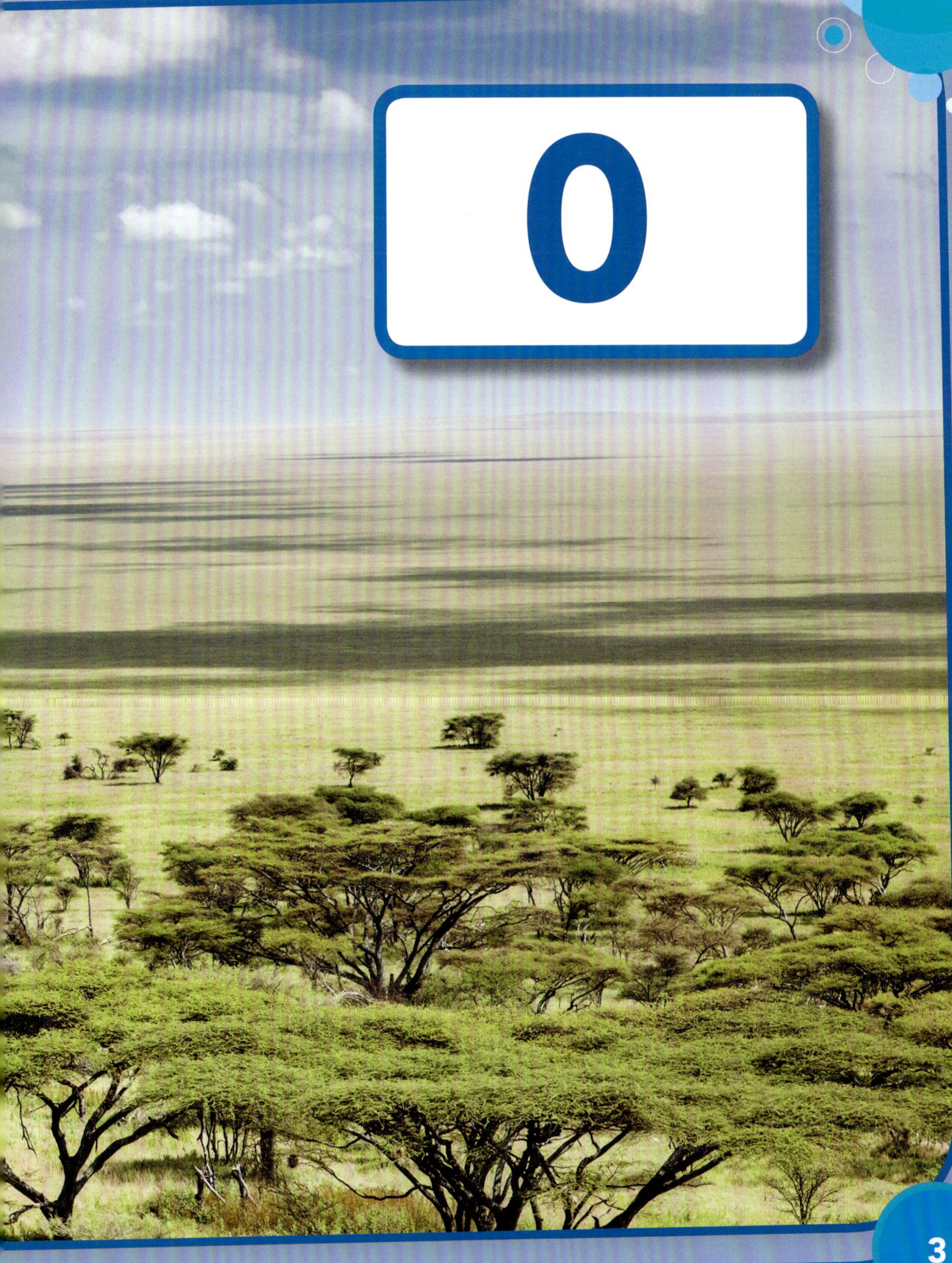

One man looks.

1

Two elephants walk.

2

Five lions drink.

5

Ten cranes fly.

10

Fifteen zebras stand.

15

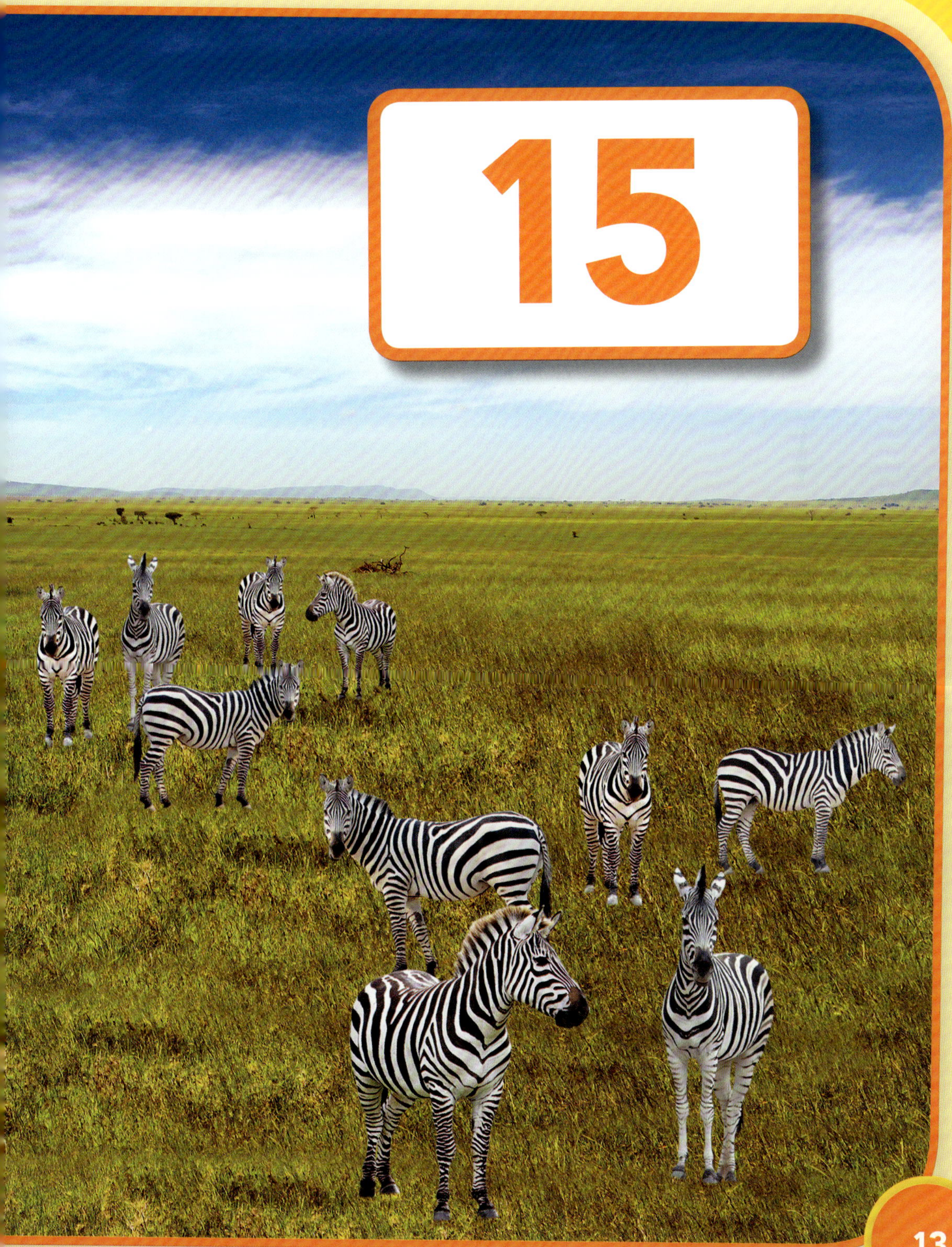

Twenty giraffes play.

20

Problem Solving

You are on safari! Count the animals you see.

1. Count the zebras.
2. Count the cranes.
3. Count the lions.
4. Count all the animals.

Answer Key

1. There are 2 zebras.
2. There are 3 cranes.
3. There are 0 lions.
4. There are 5 total animals.

Consultants

Nicole Belasco, M.Ed.
Kindergarten Teacher, Colonial School District

Colleen Pollitt, M.A.Ed.
Math Support Teacher, Howard County Public Schools

Publishing Credits

Rachelle Cracchiolo, M.S.Ed., *Publisher*
Conni Medina, M.A.Ed., *Managing Editor*
Dona Herweck Rice, *Series Developer*
Emily R. Smith, M.A.Ed., *Series Developer*
Diana Kenney, M.A.Ed., NBCT, *Content Director*
June Kikuchi, *Content Director*
Véronique Bos, *Creative Director*
Robin Erickson, *Art Director*
Stacy Monsman, M.A., *Editor*
Michelle Jovin, M.A., *Associate Editor*
Fabiola Sepulveda, *Graphic Designer*

Image Credits: All images from iStock and/or Shutterstock.

Library of Congress Cataloging-in-Publication Data

Names: Rice, Dona, author.
Title: Travel adventures : the Serengeti / Dona Herweck Rice.
Other titles: Serengeti
Description: Huntington Beach, CA : Teacher Created Materials, [2018] | Audience: K to grade 3.
Identifiers: LCCN 2017059892 (print) | LCCN 2018005968 (ebook) | ISBN 9781480759497 (e-book) | ISBN 9781425856113 (pbk.)
Subjects: LCSH: Counting--Juvenile literature. | Animals--Tanzania--Serengeti Plain--Juvenile literature. | Serengeti Plain (Tanzania)--Juvenile literature.
Classification: LCC QA113 (ebook) | LCC QA113 .R49585 2018 (print) | DDC 513.2--dc23
LC record available at https://lccn.loc.gov/2017059892

Teacher Created Materials
5301 Oceanus Drive
Huntington Beach, CA 92649-1030
www.tcmpub.com

ISBN 978-1-4258-5611-3

Printed in China WAI002